# ACKNOWLEDGEMENT

This book has been a long time coming and almost didn't quite make it but thanks to many loved one's support and belief in me…Here it is, and I know you will enjoy it and will be thirsty for more. Before I go any further, I thank God for my journey and the woman it's made me into today. I need to thank my loving brothers, sisters, my daddy, my mommy, children, grandchildren, and some special nieces and nephews. They all deserve special thanks for their patience and understanding. While I continue to grieve mommy's passing, writing this book has been some sort of way to get me through some of my hard times and my way of mourning. Next, my best friends Sharon McCormick "Bal", Dennis Allen. They have been my motivators and inspiration all my life and even though we don't talk all the time they know I love and thank them very much. Also, I cannot leave out a special friend and brother, Mark Jones Sr. You, too, have been an inspiration in my life. We don't always see things the same, but we respect each other's ideas, strengths, weaknesses and still come back to our love for each other. Thank you to all of you for allowing me to be me and accepting the good and the bad... Mostly bad! Also, thanks Mark for the art.

I am very blessed to have so many positive people in my life. They always see the best in me while I am always being my biggest critic. They've all motivated me in their own unique way but always exactly what I need at that time. Sometimes I don't like their "unique way", but I know they love me, so I listen and sometimes they may be right.

I dedicate this book to my parents, Sallie and Frank. They have always motivated and encouraged me and my brothers to try to be the best at whatever we do in life. A year before her passing, my mom told me how proud she was of me and how I was always doing something different, whether other people agreed with it or not. I know both my parents are very proud of me but hearing her say that made a big difference in my life. Thank you, mommy and daddy. I love you.

Finally, thank you readers. I love and appreciate you for your support and love. You will laugh, cry, gasp, look around and think twice about what you thought so get ready for a bumpy ride but hold on tight and enjoy.

So, without further ado, welcome to.......

# Multifariousness: Change of Seasons

# Chapter 1 --Patience

Mmmmm…Before I open my eyes, I feel so good so well rested. Warm but comfortable. Wait where the hell am I and who the fuck is this I feel next to me? As I slowly turn my head and realize where I am and looking at the man next to me, I wrestle with myself to keep my mouth close but all I can think of is "Shit, Lace, you did it again." I knew nothing good would come from that fourth glass of wine, but it was good, and we had fun. I catch myself thinking about how handsome he looks sleeping, snoring loud but "doable". His snore sounds like a big sexy monster…Why can't I have him again? He must have worked hard last night, and I will admit he does have "Lawd, Lawd have mercy" skills but I need to get out of here…preferably before he wakes up and decides he want a round two or is it round three, shit I don't know and honestly, I don't care. I feel well done!!

Landon Monroe Henderson is 6ft 2 and towers over my 5ft frame, he is undeniably gorgeous, intelligent and one of the most respected partners at a well-known law firm in Ohio. We met during a networking event a few years ago given by mutual friends and instantly hit it off. He needed some investment tips, so I agreed to stop by to look at his portfolio and give him some advice. We always have great conversations and before I knew it, we were watching Titanic, drinking wine and my legs wrapped around his deliciously sweaty manly body. We'd gone out a few times but usually just to a movie, lunch or breakfast but never anything hot and juicy like this before and never a real date, just friends. My two closest friends in the world love him and think he would be great for me also feel he will be another casualty of war. They're probably right...It would be nice if just once they weren't right. I don't know what's wrong with me.

"Lace, why are you getting up? Come back to bed" Monroe says in his best sexy morning yawny scratchy voice. He was sounding sexy and playful as he reached for me to pull me closer to him trying to kiss me. "Good morning, Monroe" I said in the same playful voice while pulling away from him. I always loved using his middle name, but I was upset with myself. How could I have let this happen? Monroe is a nice, considerate guy and sadly I really don't have time to invest in a new relationship with anyone right now…. I think. I mean I never seem to have time. I have two adult children, parents that depend on me to keep their life in order and three brothers that are constantly seeking advice for their personal life. I belong to the longest and oldest Sorority in the world and when I am not busy with my personal shit then somebody is calling me with their bullshit. I love all of them, but I hear that Dianna Ross song "It's my turn" in my head every day and I am taking heed and ready to jump and see where I land.  At 50, I am wanting to be left alone by everyone right now and I have really given some serious thought to getting in my red cranberry Porsche and driving away or moving to another country. Did I mention, I work full-time at the largest finance company in the world as the Chief Compliance Officer. No complaints, I've done very well for myself, but this relationship thing has me stumped.  "No, baby I really must go.  If I leave now, I can make it home in time to take a shower and still make the afternoon service at church".  I say as I am pulling my hair back into a bun and slipping on my shoes. I know some people at 2nd Mt Love Church of the Believers would call me a heathen but that's their opinion and what I do and don't do is between me and God.

Pastor Johnson starts the afternoon service every Sunday promptly at 12:30 pm so I knew I had to do at least 75 miles an hour on 77 south for me to make it home then to church on time. Fortunately, Sunday morning traffic wasn't a problem but unfortunately the speed limit was only supposed to be 60 miles per hour. I made it with time to spare and no speeding ticket. Pastor Johnson's sermon was always good but this Sunday, I found myself sitting in the pew in my own world. Wow last night must have been a lot more intense than I can remember. I guess that would explain the bites I found on my neck back and ass this morning. My hot chocolate skin tone made it difficult to see bites anywhere on my body except my breast but it's clear Monroe could not get enough of me last night and I am embarrassed to say I could still feel his print inside me, it felt good and made me shiver and squirm; I could feel a little wetness starting and it made me smile. It's a damn shame this man had the qualities most any woman would love to have around all the time but not me. Syncere and De Niro thought I was crazy. Just as we were standing for the benediction and dismissal I looked and saw Syn and De walking towards me. "Girl, what's wrong with you" Syn asked. "De and I have been over there waving and calling you for five minutes". "Yea and I've been calling you all night and morning. One of the reasons I came to the afternoon service instead of the early service was because I was hoping you were here," said De. "I'm fine I just had to work last night, and I was in a rush this morning" I said blushing. "Work last night, with who, doing what? Come on babe give it up whose life are you ruining now. Another victim...poor fool" Syn said and

9

De laughing. I rolled my eyes and annoyingly said "Landon Monroe and what do you mean victim. We are good friends, and we help each other out every now and then". They knew how I felt about Monroe and everything I have going on in my life so I hoped that would be the end of this conversation. Before I could finish my sentence, De Niro sarcastically asked, "So tell us again, what's wrong with Landon"? "I know you all seem to think it's me and maybe you are right, but I've asked God for guidance, wisdom and discernment and Landon Monroe is not the one". Lace said in a heavy breath. Syn rolled her eyes and said "The one, what's that? What exactly does that look like to you Lace? Just stop, let's go...I am so tired of you!"

## Chapter 2-Getting Started

My name is Velvet Lace. I always go by my middle name Lace because Velvet sounds like I just got off the pole and I'm waiting for my pimp to walk up on me and say, "bitch better have my money". Lace sounds so much better and more professional. I learned at a very young age that God listens and clearly talks to me. It was strange and scary at first but now I expect it. As a child, I'd go to church with my parents and always had questions about "the performances" people would put on in church. Was I the only one who noticed that every Sunday at 1:30 pm one of the sisters would jump up and start hollering and screaming. How did the organ player know that the Holy Spirit would be there at 1:30 pm every Sunday and he should start playing the organ louder and the pastor would start stuttering and hollering. Being friends with the pastor's kids and being accepted by the in crowd of the church was the greatest honor. You had to wear red on women's day, purple on men's day, yellow for nurse's anniversary, white for the usher board and gold and silver for the pastor's anniversary. Most importantly, your pastor, first lady and their children had to live better than everyone in the congregation at the expense of the congregation. All of this confused me, and I didn't want any parts.

As an adult I promised myself that I would never fall victim to the color game or buy myself or my children some big elaborate ensemble just to wear on Easter Sunday. I knew God existed, but I also knew that this show would not get me into heaven. I guess I was always a little bit of an arrogant rebel.

The man I married at 18 was very handsome in a "pretty boy" sort of way, Geoffrey Penn Sr aka Jeff. Women would literally stop and stare when we walked down the street, and my 17-year-old brain thought I was in heaven. Jeff could sing and that was just enough to him getting the panties much sooner than he deserved. I was also on a rebound from an ex-boyfriend, so I was on a mission to forget him, not fall in love and get married. I had completely different plans and marriage or having children was never a part of my plans. Him and I came from totally different backgrounds, I was raised Baptist, and he was raised Pentecostal. The first time I went to church with Jeff, it scared the hell out of me. I'd never seen people running up and down aisles, screaming and speaking in some type of foreign language. I mean how was the congregation supposed to know what they were talking about?? The bishop used words during his sermon, and I had no idea what he was talking about and was getting a little upset about of this craziness. I was an intelligent young woman, but I needed a translator, thesaurus and a dictionary to understand the sermon. I looked around and wondered if any of these people really knew what he was talking about, especially the elderly people who could barely read. This type of worship could not be for me, and I wondered how it could be for him. As time went on, I noticed it was more than just our religious background that was different. Our entire upbringing was totally different, and I began to wonder how a lot of things could be for him but I totally looked over those red flags.

Against my better judgement, lack of common sense and just the desire to be grown we were married in 1981. Well, 19 years later, two children, verbal, physical, mental abuse, infidelity and substance abuse, were divorcing time. My marriage was both a blessing and a curse. My ex-husband was in the military, so I lived in Germany, Japan, Philippines and France but most importantly we had to grow up real fast. He was the baby with four sisters, and I was the middle child of four brothers. You could not get any more spoiled than the two of us and we both loved it. His paternal side of the family hated me...I could not believe nor understand why but when I found out I could not respect them anymore. They were dark skinned black people who hated their own skin color, so they hated me too. No other reason they just hated me is because they hated my skin color. Even though we were together, I always wondered if he was just being rebellious when he married me. His narcissistic characteristics became our norm, and I just became conditioned to not seeing them and just accepting them as a way of marriage. I was on birth control pills, and they worked very well. In 1988 we decided to have a child, and I thought it was a fantastic idea and just what we needed to fix our deteriorating marriage. In between his substance abuse, controlling and manipulating ways we somehow managed to get me pregnant. Dream come true it was NOT! He stressed me out so much during my pregnancy you would've thought he was in labor for nine months. I was working at an eye doctor's office at the time and one morning he slapped me so hard you could see his handprint on my face. A coworker saw my face and suggested I put ice on my face before patients started coming in for the day. FYI…we were having a fun filled pillow fight and I must've hit him a little too hard with the fluffy pillow, so he slapped the hell out of me. I remember feeling so confused, crying and looking at my red face. I still don't understand. My delivery was hell, but she was beautiful. He cried and told me how much he loved me and how sorry he was for every bad thing he'd ever done wrong to me. Kelly was less than a year old when I left him and went to my parent's home. He was taking care of the drug dealer's home while his home was lacking everything. I had to go back to work earlier than I planned and tried to go back to school to finish with my bachelor's degree. I say tried because he did everything to discourage me and break down my self-esteem. Thankfully I had my family to help with my daughter while I worked and took classes while (I thought) Jeff was working. One night I got out of class, called home and a strange voice answered the phone. It was his friend from work telling me Jeff had a drug problem and must leave for treatment right now. The EAP at his job planned for him to leave on a flight going to Arizona to be admitted in a drug rehabilitation program for three months. I caught the bus in the middle of the night and was met with no lights or gas at my house…. How convenient for him! This bastard had not paid for the electricity or gas and has left me with my baby to figure things out. He worked 40+ hours a week and told me he was paying the bills. Where was his money? Stupid, silly me...I didn't know you could get drugs on credit, nor did I know the warning signs of an addict The term "functional addict" was new to me. Our home was paid for so fortunately, there was no mortgage or rent to pay. I cried for days in a freezing home taking cold baths in the dark. I could not tell anyone what was going on and no one had a clue about the misery I was living with every day when I went to work and school. I sat by the window every day on the bus headed to work so I could look out the window and no one could see me crying. I kept trying to figure out what I had done to someone in life to deserve all this pain. I kept asking God to forgive me for whatever it was, and I'd repent.

With the help of guardian angels at the electric and gas company I was able to start service in my name at the house and stupidly I missed my husband after about a month and a half. He came home with a 12-step program "a new way of life" he called it.  He went to meetings every day and lived, ate and shit this "new way of life" and I believed he changed, and I got pregnant again. Our son, Geoffrey Penn Jr. was born, and I didn't want any more children so immediately got my tubes burned, cut and told the doctor he could remove them and donate them to science. Within 5 years, Jeff had been back to treatment two more times and became more abusive. I was depressed, my self-esteem was plummeting, but I kept my head up, continued to smile and I refused to let my parents or friends know that my husband was a loser. Now that I think about it, they already knew and that's why my mom and dad always babysit my kids so I could work and go to school. Even our divorce was a struggle. Jeff didn't want anyone to say I divorced him so he refused to sign the papers, and we had to wait until he initiated and paid for the divorce so he could say he divorced me. Great just go to hell and let me be free of him.

Since my divorce, I've had to learn and accept a lot of truths about myself. Mostly great stuff, but some really fucked up mess. When I was married, my ex-husband tried to make me feel uncomfortable with myself to boost his ego. I knew I was intelligent, and beautiful but he wanted me to feel he was doing me a favor. I discovered he was insecure and jealous of my intelligence, security, family relationship and my confidence. He tried to break me down to nothing and always tried to prevent me from doing things to improve myself. He cheated on me all the time and had children by different women even before I had my children. I learned about the other kids from his mother before she died. He was living with another woman and out of town at yet another treatment center, one weekend I packed up me and my children's stuff and moved the fuck out. I'd planned it for months, so I had beds for me and my children, a few pieces of furniture and peace of mind. I moved and gave him no indication of where I had moved. I didn't take any furniture or anything from the house we lived in together I just wanted a divorce and to get far away from his trifling ass. That was the beginning of Lace again! No more caring about what anybody else thought or wanted. From that point on me and my children were my only priorities and fuck anyone who weren't on Team Lace. People call me arrogant, bougee, stuck up…mostly women…. but I am ok with all of that because it's me being confident and knowing my struggle. Now I live how I choose, like it or not. I finished school with a doctorate in Leadership and travel when and where I want. Unfortunately, usually I travel alone but it's not all bad.

I've been divorced for over 20 years and have only been in one real relationship. It lasted for five years but not with someone I would have ever given a second look. He was nice and all but not the smartest cookie in any box. People kept telling me I needed to lower my expectations and standards and go with it. Give him a chance…So I did! He was the sweetest, most irritating, little dick, couldn't fuck or even give head right man I've ever fucked. We did everything together…. shopped, traveled, at my house every day and most nights. Anything I wanted or he thought I needed he would get me. He made me feel good as a friend, but I was not attracted to him like I really should have been. We had a very bad break up.  We harassed each other and made each other's life miserable until we talked, and we are at least friends now.

"Oh well maybe it's for the best" Syncere said as one of her admirers pays her $500 speeding ticket. Syn was intelligent and gorgeous. She understood being independent didn't mean she didn't want or need a man. She was very domestic, knew how to make her man scream her name in different languages, make sure their family and finances were on point, still be submissive to her man and could cook like nobody's business. She was every insecure woman's nightmare and every man's fantasy and fear. The way she sashayed into the room full of confidence with her dark brown skin always radiant made people always wonder what's her story and either they want to fuck her or cut her. The diva was the full package, and she knew it. Below all that beauty was a fun-loving black woman that, with Gods help and direction, made it through the trenches and came out on top. A loyal friend to the end unless she is crossed and then you are merely a plaything..." for entertainment purposes only"! Syncere and Lace had been like sisters since elementary school and would fight and die for each other.

When the weather is nice, Syncere runs four miles in the morning before heading to work. She is a Vice President of the Media Department at an international internet company. Her job was stressful but it's what she wanted, and she worked hard to get what she wanted. Today was no different except when she got back to her home and ran up the stairs De was just coming out the bathroom and heading down to the kitchen. De and Syn were not officially a couple, but they were fire in the bed and everything else they did together, a real team. They met each other through Lace in Jr. high school and the three of them became best friends. Lace knew about their undercover relationship but neither of them ever talked about it nor was there any public display of affection between the two.

As De left the house, he grabbed Syn and gave her a deep wet kiss. "Mmmm, I love the way you taste after a workout" De tells Syn. She loves the way he tastes too, and his kisses are spectacular. Syn is always so horny after a morning run and the opportunity to be fucked afterwards does not happen as often as she would like. Her breathing grows faster, and she feels him growing and pressing against her. She cannot stand it anymore and begins to undress and pull De down to the floor. She straddled him and rode his hardness in her until they were both grabbing and kissing each other like they were starving and could not survive without a fix. He grabbed her and she screamed "yes harder please, I want you to cum in my pussy." "It's your dick, fuck it" he growled.

Kissing, biting, licking, sucking …it didn't matter what or how they touched each other because they felt good with each other, trusted each other and there were no boundaries with them. They screamed and climaxed so hard and passionately. They lay there shaking and still deeply kissing each other lying in their own wetness. De and Syn showered together and happily left heading to work. They both knew they were fantastic together but could not be together, right now.

Syn and De worked for the same company but in a different department, so it wasn't unusual for them to see each other several times a day. But it was difficult for them to keep their hands, tongues and bodies off each other all day, every day. She hated it but since they both had so much going on at home, most times, seeing each other at work was all the time they had together. It wasn't uncommon for their time to be very limited, so they loved and enjoyed anytime they shared, uninterrupted.

Syn was beginning to feel frustrated with that but wasn't

sure how to handle it or if was worth even discussing it

with De. I mean, what could or would change…I mean

isn't he already giving all he could to our relationship?

He'd always say just be patient and she was trying but

sometimes she wasn't sure. "Good morning, Lace" Syn

answering her cell phone.

DeNiro knew he was in love with Syncere. She was everything he'd always wanted in life and thought he was getting when he married Gwendolyn 35 years ago. Even though he and Syn met in Jr High, they were just friends, and both dated other people. He met Gwendolyn when he went to Atlanta for a family reunion one year. She lived in Cincinnati Ohio, so they kept in touch, went to Ohio State together and got married when she got pregnant in her sophomore year of college. He was always taught by his dad to take care of his children and women, so he stepped up and did what he felt was the right thing. De and Gwendolyn were married. Syn and Lace never really liked her, but they would always support their friend's decision. After a while he loved her but questioned himself about whether she was really what he wanted in a woman or his wife. He knew she wasn't but maybe she could be molded into what he needed and maybe he could be satisfied. After all Gwendolyn loved DeNiro so of course she wanted the best for her family. Before he knew it years slipped by, and they were having their fourth child. It didn't matter now what she was and wasn't, he would always be there as a provider, protector and friend. Gwendolyn knew she had a good man, and she knew he would not leave her. DeNiro was not in love with Gwendolyn, and he wished he could feel the same for her as he did with Syn.

DeNiro was four years Syncere's junior, but he was just as ambitious and mature. De was 6ft 2in, had a dark caramel complexion, beautiful eyes and perfect full lips. Their conversations could go from talking about Paris to the Garden of Eden to aliens in one sitting and neither of them would ever skip a beat. He was easy to love and to talk to. There was always some type of tension between

De and Syn and he knew why. She was intelligent, classy, sexy, confident, funny and she made him feel like no one ever had in his life. They were so much alike and a mirror of each other at times. They could have something great together. He loved just about everything about her and sometimes he wished he could take her home with him and be her knight in shining armor. He could see in her eyes she wanted to take care of him, and he felt the same way about her. But, not right now, he'd always say.

# Chapter 5—It's Time

"Hey babe" De said seeing Syn walking through the hallway. He loved watching her walk, especially in heels. The other women at their company tried to emulate her walk and style but they could not match the way her thick sexy legs met her curvaceous ass and swung back and forth, effortlessly, with every graceful movement. She was impressive and he was so proud to know she was his woman. He'd been having some thoughts about their forbidden relationship and times like these confirmed for him that he had to make some hard decisions. He couldn't deal with the hurt and tears, but he knew the time was coming for a major change for both. "I was just heading to your office to run some ideas by you for this new marketing project and see if you have time for lunch today. " De is the President of the Marketing Department and there is always something exciting going on in his department. Also, Syn and De worked hand in hand all the time when a new project comes up. Even though Syn was VP of her department, the President of Media was grooming her for his position since he would be retiring in six months, so she had free reign and made all the final decisions.

"Ok walk with me to drop this paperwork off to Stephanie and we can talk" Syn said giggling. Stephanie is one of the secretaries in the Social Awareness department and has always had a crush on De. Most women don't take a liking to Syn, especially before they know me, but Stephanie had a special kind of hate towards her. "Good morning, Stephanie" Syn said. "Good morning De Niro how are you today. That is a beautiful shirt and tie ensemble you're wearing today but then again you always dress so nice" Stephanie said. "Thank you, Syn gave it to me for my last birthday. Did you notice her dress matches what I have on today" he said tauntingly. "Oh yes I can see that, I thought maybe it was a gift from your wife or one of your children" she said with a you can't have him either grin on her face. Oh, but she was very wrong. I could have him and I would as soon as we got back to my office and locked the doors. Syn's office was at the end of a long quiet hallway, in a closed off corner so most people would call before they stopped by her office because they could not tell whether she was there or not until she answered her door. There were four offices on the floor, including her boss and he lived in California, so he was never at this location. The other two people doors were always closed too, and most people took the elevator to the 12th floor so you would always hear the elevator ring when someone arrived at the floor. De's office was not as private so usually they had meetings in Syn's office. I will admit De is a very handsome and sexy man. De is not your normal everyday man but there was something intriguing and sad about this man I loved and admired. I felt honored, in a strange and sick way, to be the woman he chose to share his love. He took pride in everything he did, and his family was his priority in life. He was a man's man. He was a protector, provider and a fixer for everyone except himself. He wasn't happy and he was only existing for everyone else. I wanted his happiness to begin and end with me. I had to sadly remind myself it didn't matter because he was and would be married and one day, probably sooner than I thought, we would have to end our relationship.

"Hey Lace, what's going on sis" De hollered toward Syn's cell. "Just calling to see what's up for lunch or dinner today with Syn" says Lace. "You can't have her for lunch or brunch, but she can probably slide you in for dinner" he said while kissing Syn on the neck. "Is everything ok or is this just a girl pow wow type thing"? He asked, knowing he could not go with them for dinner this evening. Gwendolyn just got back from visiting the kids. They all live in Miami Florida and wanted both to come down for a visit. He could not make it, but she was gone for a full seven days, and he spent every minute with Syn. "Yes, sir everything is ok and yes just a girl pow wow thing. Syn you've got my keys and the alarm code so you can come whenever, and we can cook instead of going out. I will be home about 5:30". Lace replied. Lace lives closer to Syn's job so Syn stays the night at her house during bad weather all the time. "Ok I will stop at my place and get some clothes for tomorrow and be there about 6:00" Syn excitedly said. "De you know you are always invited too" Lace says. "I know but Gwen just got back this afternoon, and she already called me to make sure I am coming straight home. She's got something planned but next time" De said lovingly It was obvious that Gwen didn't really like Syn or Lace, but she tolerated both. She always thought that there was something going on with Lace and De but she could never quite figure it out. She felt Syn was too strong and too mature for her husband so she never gave her a second thought. Contrary to her belief, the combination of Syncere's strength, tenderness, security and self-assurance were all turn-ons for her husband. Her age was a plus because she had no inhibitions and was open to new things and they taught each other a lot. Gwendoly was invited to hang out with the three of them several times, but she always declined, and no one complained.

"Hey girl" they both said while hugging when Syn came into the kitchen. Lace was finishing up her famous pasta salad and grabbing a bottle of white wine to open. "Hold up sis you know this is a school night and we both gotta still get up for work in the morning" Lace said as Syn pulled out some edibles. "Yea I know but it's still early and we need to do some serious talking tonight" said Syn as she began to set the table and take the grilled chicken breast and shrimp out of the oven. "Any way neither one of us has to punch a clock so we will be on time". She says in a sassy sarcastic tone. They talked about work, the gym, friends and relatives during dinner. Once they finished cleaning up the kitchen, they sat on the floor next to the couch with wine glasses in one hand and putting an edible in their mouth with the other hand.

"So have you talked to Landon since last week" Syn asked Lace hoping that maybe they were seeing each other. Landon was accustomed to women throwing themselves at his feet, but he was tired and wanted a real woman. He really liked Lace, and she liked him, but she always pushed him away. She would never admit it, but Syn and De knew she was afraid to make a serious commitment to anyone again because of her fucked-up marriage. She always said she wanted a monogamous relationship with a man that is physically and emotionally available, but she wasn't physically and emotionally available to a man and she has no idea where to start. Hell, if the perfect man knocked on her door right now, she would say he chews funny and sabotage that relationship. She had a way of pushing away men that could possibly meet her standards and went for the unavailable men that she knew just wanted sex or play the "boyfriend girlfriend game". She doesn't know Syn and De knows, but she even dated that self-righteous, narcissist less than a man that lives across the street from her…oh yea and married.  I want to say it was just good sex because every time we see him all we heard was Pammy this and Pammy that. I mean no problem with you loving your wife and being proud of her, but I am willing to bet my whole bank account that wasn't your story when you were trying to get the panty draws!  We hated all this for her because she deserved so much more but just settled for the scum that wasn't worth the time of day and Lace knew it was all true.  "No, I haven't seen or talked to him since that Sunday morning I saw you and De at church.  He's left several messages, but I just haven't had time to call him back" Lace whispered in a very nonchalant tone trying to pretend she could not care less…which was an untruth.  I mean what was she so busy doing…work, gym, grandkids and adult children when and if she felt like being bothered, I mean really what was she so busy doing??? Syn wondered "Remember the guy I told you I met at the Vegan restaurant a few weeks ago? The one that's a district manager for Trader Joe's. Well, we've gone out to the movies and dinner a few times". Lace said with a very small twinge of excitement in her voice. 'We spend a lot of fuck time at each other's house and in each other's bed" Syn perked up and excitedly said "really, when do we get to meet Mr. Trader Joe?" "Yea we don't spend a lot of out and about time meeting friends and relatives. He spends a lot of time and money traveling with his friends. I mean how much money could district manager at Trader Joe's take home"? Lace said with a questionable tone. By this time the edible and wine was beginning to settle in, and Lace was feeling more at ease with the conversation then she blurted out "Keith wants to watch me and another girl fucking each other!" Syn choked on her wine but managed to get out "WHAT" in between coughs. "I mean I don't have anything against anyone who likes that type of thing, but you don't even know him and why does he feel comfortable asking you for that anyway? What did you tell him"? "Well, I didn't say no, nor did I say yes…it was more like I said maybe" Lace said in a slightly ashamed voice. "What do you mean maybe? Is that something that you are interested in doing because you know just doing it for him will fuck you up for life. Where are you at in this relationship with this man? None of us have ever met him and you talk about him very casually like he's just a good fuck so what's really going on with you"?? Syn said in an irritated tone. Lace looked at her and angrily said "I am tired of adding to my body count and I am ready to settle down. I mean look around I am smart, beautiful, intelligent woman with a lot going for myself, but the whores and needy women are winning out here in these streets. Our parents taught us how to be a good woman but that was the definition of a good woman in the 60's, 70's, 80's and some of the 90's. I am a fantastic friend and very open minded but just not quite needy enough to make a man feel like a real man. A good woman is based on each man's definition not our definition and what we are taught or want to believe. You and I are what every man wants but afraid because they don't think we can really be what and who they see. An anomaly….is that a compliment or something? I hear that all the time so I should I be happy or proud that my anomaly ass is too good to be true so the prize I win is I get to be single…What kind of bullshit is that??? They don't believe they really can have it all in one woman so they settle for who and what they know they can control with no questions asked…. which also is the one that usually will cheat while he's busting his ass to make life better for their family. He may even cheat with the other women, but he will always be afraid to take that chance to be happy with the other woman" …as soon as Lace said that last part she wanted to take it back. She wasn't trying to hurt Syn but unfortunately that was her and De's scenario. "I've tried staying celibate and praying for my husband. I've tried stepping out on faith picking a wedding date, going to the bridal shop picking out my wedding dress, picking a hall and paying the deposit and still nothing manifested so I am not sure how agreeing to be with another woman every now and then with my husband can be any crazier." Syn's high was wearing off, so she drank the whole glass of wine with one gulp and patiently said to Lace "I understand, and you are right but make sure you are doing this because you want it not because you want him. Do you think you could be happily married to Keith"? Lace hesitantly replied with tears in her eyes "I don't know, and I never thought about him in a married capacity. I am just tired of the back-and-forth games and he's in the picture and he really is an intelligent, decent man. Probably eventually we could be happy."

Syn laughed and cried too now saying" You know everything you said is true and I feel the same. I love De and would go to the end of the earth for him or with him but deep down inside I always have the question of whether he would do the same for me or would Gwen always be the final deciding factor for him. Gwen not his children or family but Gwen. I wasn't going to tell you this, but I have to tell someone because I really have no one else to talk to about my relationship with De and I don't want to put you in the middle of it but me and De are meeting for dinner Sunday, and he doesn't know it but I need something more. I don't quite know what more I want or need from him, but I know this is not enough anymore. I am ready to move on without him if I must. Our relationship just doesn't give me anything I want or need anymore. It never really did but I was hoping something would change with his situation, but it hasn't, as a matter of fact it seems like it's getting worse. I mean they are getting closer. You have no idea how many men, SINGLE MEN, would love to get with me. I pray whatever happens in this relationship doesn't take away from the three of us still being best of friends, but I don't know what else to do. When I see or hear him talking to Gwen, I don't see an unhappy man. I think he is in love with her, and I am just a side chick." Lace was shocked to hear Syn say that and didn't know what to say because honestly, she really felt her thoughts about De were correct.

"Well, you know I am down with you sis and will always support you but don't get mad when I support De the same way. He is my brother you know" Lace sad with tears rolling down her face. "Why are you crying girl? You are making me cry now." Syn tearfully said "I knew one day it would come to this and I love both of you so much. I don't want to lose either of you. You two are all I have in life right now and now we possibly may not be able to be partners in crime anymore.... Damn that Gwendolyn...where did she come from anyway!!!" Hollered Lace. Syn began to walk back and forth and suddenly she realized she could lose De and there would be nothing between them. She felt like a fool. She was a very intelligent woman, and she knew that a married man had nothing to offer her but maybe a hard dick. He could not spend time with her when she needed him, and she

could never depend on him for absolutely anything.

When her mom passed, he was one of the first ten people

she contacted thinking somehow, he would be there to

comfort her. He wasn't there to hold her while she cried

and screamed or to listen to her when she just needed to

talk about her mom.  I didn't see him and his wife until

the end of the service at my mom's Homecoming service

as they were leaving out of the church for maybe two

minutes…possibly less.  No matter how much he said, "I

love you", he had really never shown her anything to

prove it, and I guess she'd never really put those

demands on him.  It always bothered her when he was

always at Gwen's undeserving silly beck and call

sometime immediately after they'd made love. Syn hated

it but she continued because she loved him.  How could

she possibly be expected to see him every day at work

and just act like none of this ever happened. Oh my god, could he act like nothing ever happened between us…. that would crush her.   Will she have to quit her job, maybe move to another city. Syn started to cry uncontrollably.  Grant it she was buzzing a little but she was beginning to see the reality of all of this "Oh my god, I love this man and I never thought about how my life would be without him.  Lace, what am I going to do? Why didn't you stop me? I am not ready to lose him, but I cannot keep allowing myself to be in this painful relationship!" Lace was stunned and she had never seen Syn act like this before.  Even when her mom passed a few years ago she didn't break down like this. She didn't have words to say or had any idea what she should be saying to her best friend.  Lace grabbed Syn and they just sat on the floor rocking back and forth crying until they both fell asleep.

# Chapter 7—Office Drama

The next day was Friday, and the air was very heavy between De and Syn at work. You could scoop up the air with a plastic spoon. There was so much frustration and tension between the two of them for no good reason at all. They didn't have a disagreement, and they were cordial towards each other a little too cordial. None of this came from De but from Syn. She knew how she felt and what she had to talk to De about and she was nervous about the discussion, De's reaction and response to this conversation would affect her and their relationship. Syn finished her work for the day and decided to start her weekend early. De saw her head toward the door and grabbed her hand and went in for a big hug and seductive kiss. "Hey babe where have you been all day and where are you going?" De asked with a sexy concerned voice. He knew she was upset about something and was puzzled about whether he could help and why she was pulling away from him while he was trying to hold her. This was a hallway that no one ever used with no cameras. One time he gave her head in this very hallway. He loved the fact that they could share and do any and everything together. There was never any judgement from either of them and they felt comfortable and secure with each other. He wished he could get this at home but that would never happen with him and Gwen. He saw Syn earlier with a real fucked up look on her face and wondered what was wrong with her. He was headed to her office to check on her since she had not answered his calls earlier. Syn loved the way he held and kissed her, but she had to pull away a little after kissing him back "I am just headed home early. I meant to call you back, but I got really busy trying to finish up. Lace and I had a bit too much to drink last night and I didn't sleep well on her floor last night" she said holding her stomach and giggling at the same time. "Oh, yea I forgot you two had your girl's night out last night. Talk about me much?" He asked in a sly joking voice. Syn gazed at him and laughed "Absolutely not one word about you. You do know we have a lot of amazing things to talk about. I mean you can be amazing but not this time babe I just need to rest and clear my head." She hesitantly said to him, hoping to not sound frustrated. "Are you ok? You know I can take off too if you need me. Everything is finished on my desk and it's a long weekend, so I am ready to go anyway." he said excitedly. Syn forgot it was President's Day weekend and hoped the extra day off would make the outcome from the Sunday evening date a little easier to return to work Tuesday. "Hon what time am I picking you up for dinner Sunday or should I come over Saturday and just never leave you?" De said anxiously while kissing Syn on her neck and making a slow dance movement with her body. She swooned with him and said, "oh that sounds fantastic I'd love the latter." They kissed and agreed to if he could make it then Saturday would be great but if not then Sunday at 5pm would be good. After many more kisses Syn headed to her car and De back to his office.

While walking back to his office, De saw a familiar face. He wasn't sure but realized he was right it was the last person he needed to see and wondered why he was here and walking with the VP of the Human Resource department. It was Tyler Adams. Tyler attended the same church as him and worshipped the ground Syn walked on. He hated Tyler and loathed the way he always walked up to Syn and hugged and kissed her on the cheek. Tyler was 6 feet 3 inches, creamy dark fudge complexion, beautiful white teeth, very intelligent, no children and single. Tyler turned and saw him, reached out his hand and started to approach De. "DeNiro" he said while shaking his hand "I thought this was the firm you worked for. It's great seeing you here. Doesn't Syncere work here too? It will be great working with the two of you and being taught the industry ropes by you two. "Brent, the he head of the HR department broke in and said "it's great you two already know each other. Tyler is the new Associate Director of our Operations department. DeNiro is the President of our Marketing Department so you will be working with him closely." "Great and Syncere is the VP of Media, right? I am excited about getting a lot of input from her too." Tyler said. Brent giggled and said "for now but I expect a promotion to come Miss Syncere's way very soon so you better get in while you can." "So where is Miss Syncere, Tyler said sarcastically imitating Brent, I'd love to say hi and give her the good news too" De stand offishly answered "She went home early today, she wasn't feeling well so I guess it will have to wait until Tuesday." Suddenly De was feeling a little jealous. He knew Tyler and Syn could possibly be good together and he could offer her so much than he could. De knew of Tyler's financial investments and he noticed how attentive and attracted he was to Syn. During the days following the death of Syn's mom Tyler was at her house every day to help receive guest and to make sure she ate and rested. He helped with whatever she needed and was right next to her at the Homecoming. De had to admit Tyler was the sort of man and friend Syn deserved in her life all the time not just part time...maybe.

"DeNiro", Stephanie called as he turned the doorknob of his office door. De just wanted to make it back to the office so he could close his door and let all his calls go to voice mail since his secretary was out today. "Do you have a minute for me to talk to you," she said shyly. "Sure, my door is always open for business" De said loudly in a very professional voice. De left the door open when she sat down but Stephanie stood up and said this is private and she preferred the other employees not hear their conversation.

De said ok but was confused by her response. He could not understand what she could have to discuss with him in private. She was not his secretary and was not in his department. Maybe she wanted to discuss her job or a possible new job placement. As she sat back down in her seat, she had a very devilish expression on her face, and it almost scared De but it definitely said be afraid be very afraid. Stephanie always dressed nice, professional with a hint of sexy but today her dress and body was saying "I need to be fucked hard...thank you very much sir." She had a painted on dark blue pencil skirt on with a split so high that when she crossed her legs you could play peek a boo for days. Coochie, not coochie…. Coochie! Her powder rose blouse was just low cut enough for her deep plunge lace blue bra to accentuate her full breast and it looked exquisite next to her cocoa brown skin. Not too small and not too large but a perfect mouthful. Last, but not least, those legs…she wore rose pink heels with a blue flower clip on them. Oh my god she was beautiful, fit and on the prowl today and her victim would be De. She fantasized how gorgeous he looked standing in her home completely naked. She could almost taste him in her mouth as she swallowed all of him down her throat. She didn't care about his marriage or his relationship with Syn. The more the merrier as far as she was concerned. Oh, she had something for Syn. The first time she saw Syn and De together she knew they were a couple, and she had to have both. They looked so sexy together and they made her body hot! She fantasized about licking Syn's pussy while riding De's hard dick. No one would ever suspect that Stephanie was bisexual. She was always so girly and was always dating men...we all thought.

Stephanie noticed De looking at her legs and shyly said "How rude of me is this a good time for you right now?" De stood walking over to his office door intending to open the door but before he could reach the door Stephanie stood up in front of him and leaned her hot breast against him. She didn't intend to play games or be shy with him today. She was there for a reason, and it was time to reveal the reason. "You know De I think you are a very sexy man, and I know you are married but if you don't see that as a problem I don't either" saying seductively as she began to unbutton her blouse. She shocked De when she started to kiss him first on this cheek then his neck then his mouth. Her lips were so full and soft, and he wanted to kiss her back, but he resisted. She began to unbutton his belt buckle then unzip his pants and he tried unsuccessfully to stop her. He tried to push her back, but she pushed him back onto his desk and in one smooth movement she jerked down his pants, fell to her knees and put his fully erected dick in her mouth. She sucked, licked and he was riding her face until they were both moaning and grinding in unison. Just as he thought he could take control of the situation and stop this madness she opened her mouth wide took his balls in her mouth and started licking the area under his balls in front of his asshole. She moaned like she had a delicacy in her mouth, and she could not get enough of all of him. He stopped breathing, reached for anything to grab and gave out a loud holler as he exploded all over her face and in his mouth. He'd never felt that much pleasure in his entire life, and it scared him because he reached down to grab her face and kissed her with deep and intense passion. He loved it and knew he would want much more of that! She licked her ice cream delight clean, fixed her blouse, checked her face and hair and as she turned to leave said "let Ms. Syn know she's next on my list and we can make it a threesome." She smirked with a face of pride and accomplishment and left. De was speechless.

## Chapter 8—The Beginning?

"Hello Mr. Monroe, how are you doing today sir? I am sorry I didn't call you back when you called but I've been so busy with work and family. It's almost midnight on a Friday night and a long weekend. What are you doing up and not out kicking it with some lucky female" Lace said sarcastically answering her cell phone. She really didn't intend to answer his call, but he was so persistent, and she thought he may need some financial advice and to be honest she wouldn't be opposed to getting a piece of that tonight. "Good evening, Lace. I am sorry I didn't realize the time. I hope I didn't interrupt anything or wake you", he said partly apologetic and the other part in a curious noisy tone. Landon really liked Lace and he wished they could spend time together to really get to know each other but Lace just didn't seem to be interested in him. He always tried to spend time with her, but he just couldn't seem to get it right. He felt like she had put him in the friend zone and he's just her boy toy. "No, you didn't wake me, and I am just sitting here watching tv and reading a book by Graham Masterson. What's up?" Landon explained to her how he intended to go to the movie but started looking at his portfolio and realized some of his numbers weren't matching and weren't in line with what he was expecting. He also adamantly told her that there was no lucky woman in his life. "I didn't expect you to really answer the phone but I'm glad you did. Lace, do you know how much I enjoy the time we spend together? You are beautiful, smart, so much fun and I really feel comfortable and vulnerable with you. I've never felt like this with any other woman. I feel like I can tell you anything and not be judged." His words surprised himself and he could not believe he said those things to her, but he could not stop talking and it all felt so natural.

"Wow!" she said flattered and very surprised to hear him say those things to her. Her feelings scared her, but she decided to respond. "I've never had anyone say those things to me. I enjoy our time together too but honestly; I always thought you just thought of me of no more than a sex object. I didn't think you really cared for anything more than sex." She was a little embarrassed and sad. Could her soulmate possibly have been right here the whole time?

"Lace you are a great woman and deserve a great man to take care of you and treat you like a queen. "He began to tell her about his previous relationships with women that tried to take advantage of his kindness. He was raised by his mom and grandmothers and understood that all women want a loving man to submit to. She wants to be heard, understood, not disrespected and rescued from the world sometime.  His dad passed when he was 12 years old, but he remembered seeing his dad rub her feet or brush her hair and they talked about their vision and dreams for their family. They called themselves the MultiTwins.  They were so much alike but so different in so many ways.  They complemented each other in every way.  He wanted that type of marriage and maybe a child, but he was ok with adopting, if necessary. Lacey held the phone away from her face and made a "don't play with me look" toward the phone.  None of this could be true and this was a damn good "gettin' the panties" line but it was working on her and she was ready for all of that and more.

Lace had both her mom and dad in the household and always saw her parents working together with the finances.  They owned property and taught her and her brothers to always reach for the stars. They always instill in their children, especially their only daughter, there is absolutely nothing you cannot do or have with hard work. She knew it was difficult to find a single man with a similar background and understood the importance of working together and supporting each other to achieve something amazing. She could feel herself cozying up to Landon like you do in a big comfortable recliner with a big fluffy blanket. Suddenly she had an overwhelming warm feeling, and she felt ok with sharing her story with Landon. She still felt a little hesitant and unconsciously looked for any red flags but felt like why not see what happens and he is SINGLE!! She knew women admired Landon and she just found it hard to believe he felt like this about her. I mean why her???

They talked for hours until Landon said, "Let's meet for breakfast." Lace agreed and said, "ok we can meet in the morning". "It is morning love" Landon said. Lace opened her light blocking curtains and could see the sun rising. They'd talked all night, and it felt like time stood still. "Ok sounds great but that means we will have to hang up the phone so we can get dressed" she said laughing and partly not wanting to hangup. She didn't want this to end. Landon laughed too and said "True, how about an hour and a half at a mom-and-pop breakfast spot tucked away on Coventry. I don't remember the name, but their food is great. Make sure you wear something comfortable maybe we can catch a ferry to one of the Islands or a festival somewhere…If that's ok with you". Lace was shocked and very hesitantly said "okaaay sounds fantastic see you in an hour and a half". She hung up her phone thinking what kind of mess is this supposed to be God? I mean, is this a date? She didn't like how this made her feel but sure why not play along for now.

She arrived at the restaurant about 15 minutes early and he was already there with white, yellow and red roses. He stood up when he saw her enter the restaurant, walked over to meet her and hugged and gently kissed her on the lips. His lips never felt this good and didn't remember them being this full and soft.  Not to mention most of her dates in the past were 30 minutes late or if they were early, they'd order their food and start to eat before she could even get there. All of this was strange, and her normal reaction would have been to find something to complain about and sabotage this lovely breakfast date instead she decided to just enjoy Monroe, the food and the restaurant…. No excuses!  I don't know what's going on today, but it feels amazing.  Landon had chocolate chip pancakes, and I had French toast with berries, and we shared an order of plant-based bacon. Everything was so good, and the atmosphere and waitress was fantastic and made our date great. All the employees and customers thought we were newlyweds or had been dating for a while. They talked to us like they'd known us for years or like we were regular customers. We talked and laughed for hours and after 4 hours of this we finally decided we should at least leave the restaurant. We ain't gotta go home but we had to get up from there! It was crazy because we didn't make it far from the door before, we started laughing and talking again. This time we were standing in the restaurant's parking lot for an hour just talking. Employees came out because their shift was over and just smiled at us. Since his house was close by, we decided to park my car at his home and drive his car wherever we were going next. I expected him to tell me to park my car in the garage or on the street to prevent any girl friends from seeing an unfamiliar car in his driveway, but I was happily surprised when he didn't say anything about where I parked and insisted, I park in the driveway. He opened the door for me to get in his car, he let the top down, and we drove away with smooth jazz playing loudly in the air. I am in love.

We spent the full day together eating, going to the park, we went to the Puerto Rican Festival and danced until my feet were swelling. We finally settled down at a restaurant with a live jazz band and it seemed we were inseparable. "This has been a fairy tale day. I want to pinch myself just to make sure I am not in a dream." "I agree beautiful woman." Lance grabbed her hand and kissed it" I admit I dreaded the sunset because I don't want today to end. You are so much more than I ever imagined. I can't believe someone like you has always been right here and I never knew it. I've always prayed for a woman like you but never imagined one existed and she would be right here with me. How could you be single?" Lace could not control herself anymore and she started to cry. "I don't know why I am still single. I really think I am afraid of a real relationship and tend to sabotage things. I am afraid of being vulnerable and being hurt by someone I love again. It's amazing we've only been together for 24 hours, on the phone all night and together all day and I really feel like I've known you all my life. I feel comfortable with you and like I can trust you with my heart. Lance, I don't want to stop what we've shared today." Lance pulled her close to him, kissed her and said me either. "Are you ready to go?" When they got to his house, they both just sat in the car waiting for the other to initiate something, anything that insinuated these 24 hours would become 48 hours. Lance opened his door, stepped out of the car, walked to her side of the car, opened her door and stretched out both his arms to her. She took his hands, and he led her to his house door. They silently went into the house and that was the beginning. Their love making was different from the times in the past. They laughed, talked, sang together and made love some more. At one point, they even went into his backyard, naked, and just walked around talking and laughing. The closeness was fantastic and completely indescribable.

## 9. Is this the End?

The long weekend was just what was needed for everyone, but Lace realized she had not talked to Syn or De all weekend and she had sooooo much to tell them. They would be extremely happy for both her and Lance. Once she and Lance finally pulled themselves away from each other and finalized whose house they would be at for the rest of the week she tried to reach Syn and De. Her and Lance wanted to get together with them for dinner this week and share their good news. She tried calling them all the way to work and once she got to work several times. She remembered they had their big dinner date on Sunday and was excited to find out what happened to them. Lace walked into her job, and everyone asked her what she was doing different to her skin because she was glowing and looked like she had glitter on her face, but she did not and just told them she got a lot of rest this weekend but she knew it was the after glow of being with Landon Monroe.... She was hoping there would be messages from De or Syn but there were none and now it's 12pm and still no call from either. "Ok now I am worried" she said to herself. It's not like them to not called or at least left a message by now. Now she thought about it, neither of them returned her call when she left a message for them Sunday and Monday to let them know where and who she was with this weekend. At 2pm she could not stand it anymore and she was worried so she could not work anyway, so she packed up her briefcase, grabbed her purse and headed out the door to leave for the day. She thought she'd go to Syn's house first but then decided to stop at her house first just to look around and make sure neither of them had stopped by or was still there. Seriously, she hadn't really been at her house all weekend and they could have been there the full time. Lace jumped in her car and sped out of the parking lot of her job but as she turned the corner, she saw Gwen riding in a police car coming from the direction of Syn and De's job. We both looked at each other at the same time but I could tell she was crying. She stared at me with an indescribable expression on her face that bothered me and made me concerned and determined to find my brother and sister as fast as possible. She didn't see any sign of their cars or that they were at her home or had been there at all as she ran from room to room. Now, she would head to Syn's house but first she would call Lance to ask him to meet her there in about 15 minutes. She felt a little apprehensive and just wanted him with her right now.

"Hey babe how are you doing today hon?" She asked Lance. Right away he could hear her voice shaking and gave the phone call his full attention. She told him the full scenario, from Syn and De's affair, to as much as she knew about their Sunday date to her seeing Gwen crying in the police car. She did not know but Landon was already out of his office, in his car and headed toward Syn's house before she'd even finished telling him about the affair. He knew his woman needed him now and he had no time to make any judgments on her best friends. Lace was surprised to see Landon pull up in his car at Syn's house at the same time she did, but she was so grateful he was there to hold her no matter what was going on today. First, they walked around the outside to see if there were any forced entries or broken windows and found nothing, so they went to the front door. Lace pulled her extra key out of her purse and reached for the door. Lace started to walk away, and Landon grabbed her hand and protectively said "babe we are doing this together. I will go first, and you can follow with me."

She hesitantly nodded her head ok but the rebellious side of her said "hell no you follow me." They went from room to room in Syn's house but found no sign of either of them. It scared her but then she remembered one other place to check. A few years ago, Lace and Syn jokingly agreed to have a secret hiding place in their homes only they knew about to hide any of their undesirable sex toys, clothes, letters, notes and other things "normal people" would think as being crazy. In case of a sudden death of either of them the other only assignment would be to go to the house and go to the secret hiding place and gather all the things there before anyone could get to it. Lace jumped off the bed and ran down the hall but before she could get to the secret spot, she could see the main closet door slightly open and there it was. As she reached inside the opening, her hand got tangled in something sort of sticky on the floor. As she looked down, jumped back, she screamed and started to cry all at the same time. There on the floor next to the secret hiding spot was a letter from Syn and De. Landon Monroe read the letter with her and was more determined to be a good supportive man, now more than ever. He held her shaking body and led her down the stairs and out of the house.

Right now, life seems so different to me. Several times a day I drive by Syn's house trying to put things together. I have so many questions for both Syn and De…I just don't understand what happened and why they did not tell me…They didn't trust me. I don't know whether to fuss and hate them or just try to understand their position in this whole situation and love them. A few times, Gwendolyn tried to reach out to me for information, but I hate her and refused to talk to her. She was going through a different type of hell and confusion right now and I could be of no help.

I will admit I had a lot of confusion and unanswered questions, especially when I ran into Tyler and Stephanie at the mall. I remembered Syn talking about Stephanie, but I didn't think her and De knew Tyler and Stephanie were such good friends. Neither of them seemed to be upset or curious. I thought that was strange and just as I was about to start my questions, Monroe called, and they quickly walked away laughing like they had a secret that they knew I didn't know.

Made in the USA
Columbia, SC
05 November 2024

45453914R00043